A BRIDLED AFFAIR

WHEN LOVE IS A GAMBLE

DE DE COX

A BRIDLED AFFAIR

Male Model:	Scooter Minyard
Assistant:	Jeanette Moore
Photographer:	Austin Ozier / Medici Creative
HMUA:	Scooter Minyard
Wardrobe:	Scooter Minyard
Venue:	Wagner's Pharmacy

Quantity sales and special discounts are available on quantity purchases by corporations, associations, and others. For details, contact the publisher at the address above.

U.S. trade bookstores and wholesalers, email info@BeyondPublishing.net to place an order.

The Beyond Publishing Speakers Bureau can bring authors to your live event.

For more information or to book an event, contact the Beyond Publishing Speakers Bureau at speak@BeyondPublishing.net

The author can be reached directly at BeyondPublishing.net

Printed in the United States of America. Distributed globally by BeyondPublishing.net

BEYOND
PUBLISHING

New York | Los Angeles | London | Sydney

ISBN Softcover: 978-1-63792-680-2
ISBN Hardcover: 978-1-63792-679-6

DEDICATION

I remember the year. I remember the event. It was the beginning of Derby season. Lord, he was the one that everyone spoke about when it came to fashion shows. I had seen his work on social media. I did not know how it would happen, but I knew I was going to meet him. I knew he was going to change my life, but the magic was, I had no idea how he would impact my life.

My best friend, Eileen Hornback, and I love and still do, all the events leading up to Derby. There was a fashion show that had been scheduled at the Kentucky Derby Musuem and he was the ONE directing and producing, but the best part, he was showcasing his designs.

As soon as we walked in and took our seats, it was magical. From beginning to end, you knew he was a phenom. At the end of the show, he paused. He spoke about the models, designers, volunteers, supporters, friends, AND then he stopped. He looked down from the stage and began the words that would change my life - "thank you to my mom". He stepped off the stage, walked towards her, and knelt down. Her arms stretched towards him. She was so petite. He wrapped his arms around her and kissed her.

Love has no bounds. Love is endless. Love was what I witnessed, in its truest form. The love between a child and a parent. The love between a son and his mother.

He has been with me for over ten years and has been the official HMUA and now cover model of my romance books for over four years. God's blessings come when you least expect them. God's blessings come when you feel you do not deserve them. This is how I think of Scooter Minyard. A blessing given to me by the good Lord.

I am prayerful he knows how much I genuinely love him. Not because of his talent or expertise or good looks but because he understands what love truly is ... unconditional! (Acts 20:35)

PROLOGUE

Sitting in the restaurant watching the cook, Jimmy, get down to the business of orders, Callan Duncan, knew who would be the next to walk in. Habits are hard to change. Habits are more difficult to change as you age. Callan knew this because he was a prodigy of habits. It began with his grandfather and transferred to Callan's father and Callan's father made sure that Callan would not forget.

Jimmy turned around and said, "Here's your usual. Eggs, toast, and coffee. Just out of curiosity, Callan, have you ever considered adding a bit of spice to your life?"

Callan looked at Jimmy and smiled. Jimmy had been a part of Callan's life beginning at birth. From the car seat to the barstool, this was all Callan had known about his grandfather and father. Callan's mother had died during childbirth, and it was just the "guys".

Jimmy commented, as he turned from laying the silverware down for Callan, "it's hard not to think about him and this day, isn't it?"

Callan nodded. "Yes. This was the day a piece of my life was ripped from me. My life has changed. I'm not a gambling man, but I never understood until now how the odds of fate work."

Jimmy nodded. He knew what that statement meant, especially coming from Callan Duncan. I understand. "Best hurry up and finish before the 'usuals' come in and require your insight into the day."

Callan laughed. "Yes, Jimmy. Have I ever let you or them down?" Jimmy chuckled and turned back to the grill. Callan knew he should count his blessings. Jimmy had been the one constant in Callan's life since Callan had lost his father. As Callan took his last sip of coffee, the door opened and Callan heard the words that would begin his day, "Who's running today, Callan?"

CHAPTER 1

There is an old saying that life can change in a second. Callan Duncan knew this saying well and had personally experienced that second. Callan Duncan also knew that life could change on the wrong pick. Win, place or show were the only options. These three words would haunt Callan late at night. He really had no choice when it came to his "gift".

Reaching for the necklace, Callan placed his hand on each item. Callan did not know why it was so important to make sure, but he needed reassurance that they were still there. If you were at a distance, the naked eye would not catch or have no clarity of what was held so close to his chest.

Callan never took it off. He could not. Callan needed security. These mementos were his constant companion. Whenever Callan was in doubt about a decision made, he reached for the three pennies. He could rub his thumb over each. Each penny revealed a specific date. Underneath the pennies, was where a small medallion lay and the words "lucky" engraved. This one word held Callan's fate in the industry.

Walking towards the table his father had occupied and helped others understand the industry, Callan knew that life could change on a gamble as well. He really had no choice in his career path.

Sitting at this table with his father, Callan had received the education and knowledge (not just of his father) but of those colleagues in the industry. Callan had learned to read and add. His schoolteachers were astonished at how well Callan mastered both at such a young age, especially in both subjects.

If Callan's secret had been revealed, he was confident child protective services would have been contacted. But instead, Callan excelled in school. Math was nothing but numbers. This was the environment he had been raised in since he could talk. His father had placed the program book in Callan's hands and told him to open it. It did not matter which page. Callan needed to learn to read a program and recognize numbers associated with each jockey and the horse.

Many weekends were spent at the restaurant, listening to his father and grandfather talk about the next best thing coming to the track. Circumstances, fate, tradition and even luck would determine the outcome of the win. Callan's grandfather and father were survivors of the unknowns. Callan, on the other hand, was gifted.

As Callan matured in comprehension of the industry, he surpassed the reputation of both his grandfather and father. Callan had never questioned his path that both had placed his feet on. At times it had been rocky, but the road or the track would eventually lead Callan to victory.

Callan was observing the regulars as they walked in to sit and shoot the breeze before heading out to the track. But today was different, not because of the anniversary of losing his father, but Callan felt uneasy. He could feel it in the air. He reached for the cup of coffee he had brought to his table.

Allie, who was Jimmy's girlfriend and a permanent staple in the restaurant, approached and asked if he needed a refill or just to top it off.

Callan winked and said, "I only need you, Allie."

Allie smiled. "Honey, you couldn't handle me. Finish your coffee and don't be late for the first race." When Jimmy had first introduced Allie, Callan immediately knew she would be the mother type, matriarch of the restaurant.

Allie knew every single customer or tourist, for that matter, that walked through the restaurant doors. For some, opening the door was a new beginning. For others, it was home.

When Callan had lost his father unexpectedly, Allie was the one constant in his life. Callan could have lost sight of his destiny or the gift. It could have happened to him because of this tragic event, but Allie had stepped in and made sure that did not happen. Callan had been told the gift was a blessing. He was lucky to have both.

Looking at the doors, preparing to leave, Callan still did not feel lucky nor blessed. He still had yet to see the big picture.

Allie stood at the counter watching Callan. She took a drink of her coffee. Jimmy leaned through the pick-up counter. "Is he ready. Are the picks chosen?"

Allie leaned backwards to acknowledge Jimmy's question. "He's good. In all of the uncertainty and with today's special significance, he's confident. I told him my favorites." Jimmy's eyebrow rose. "And did you tell him mine, Allie? Does he know who my favorites are?"

"Yes, sugar, he knows your favorites. He's been fed. He's been topped off with coffee. There's nothing holding him back."

Jimmy tilted his head. "Then why is he still sitting."

Allie smiled. "I don't know."

CHAPTER 2

Opening the door to walk outside to head to the gates, Callan heard, rather than saw, the voices of the conversation. He saw a man in similar age to his own father. He was reaching for the young woman's hand. She pulled it away.

She turned in Callan's direction. He stopped. Her stare was haunting. She was hurting. Callan knew this look. He was not new to the look of disappointment. He could not turn away. He knew the direction he needed to walk to start his day. And it was nowhere near her. Without giving thought to what he would do, Callan took the first step.

Nova was embarrassed. There were just times that she could not control her disbelief of the circumstances that were surrounding her and her father. This was one of those moments. She thought she had kept her voice down. Evidently not. Because now there was a stranger observing her.

Nova could tell he wanted to say something. She could also tell by his stride that he was unsure if he wanted to say anything. Better to let him off the hook and steer him in the direction away from her and her father. Nova raised her hand to wave him off. Still, that did not stop his forward motion.

Nova's father looked out of the corner of his eye. Callan knew he was eyeing him up. "We are fine, son. My daughter and I are just having a brief discussion regarding our family business."

Callan threw his hand up. "Just checking, sir, to be sure the young woman did not need any help." Callan tilted his head. "Are you okay, miss?"

Nova chuckled. She looked at her father. "Well, are you going to repeat it again?" Murray inquired. Nova's father, Murray, again reached for her hand. Callan noticed she did not pull it away this time. "Sir, I can assure you I am fine. This is my father, Murray Cross. I am Nova Cross, his daughter. He and I were just discussing the day's events. You possibly could have heard my tone of disagreement."

Callan busted out laughing. She had such a nonchalant approach to Callan's concern. "Well, now that you mention it," Callan began, "I was a tad bit concerned, but I'm going to assume everything is under control?"

Murray Cross winked. "Don't let her charm scare you away. She's concerned that I'm not thinking clearly when it comes to our race today. I can assure you that I am aware of the competition that our Betty Boots will encounter."

Nova glared at her father. "Dad, that's enough. We don't even know him." Callan didn't know who had pissed on her teddy bear, but someone certainly had. She was not giving an inch with any more information.

Callan held his hand out. "My name is Callan Duncan. I have not seen you around here before." Callan knew that Mr. Cross would return the gesture. The daughter on the other hand was a totally different story. Callan noticed his daughter, Nova, was not keen on the exchange. "Don't worry. I know when I have my marching papers. I hope you both have a great day. Who knows, I may see you today?"

As Mr. Duncan was speaking to Nova, her eyes were immediately drawn to his chest. How could it not be? He looked like a magazine cover model. His attire was not that of a typical racetrack attendee nor of any trainer. His shirt was unbuttoned just enough to tease the eyes of any woman who may wonder what lie under the shirt. He was wearing a necklace of some kind. It looked as though there was a medallion and possibly some type of coin or coins. She could not remove her eyes from his chest. If she stared much longer, Callan Duncan would surely notice her obvious curiosity. Or, he would think she had no manners and was plain rude.

Nova could tell that this Callan Duncan was trying to make cordial. She was not impressed. So many had tried to get to her through her father. Nova knew his type when she saw it. He was carrying the racetrack program rolled tight in one hand. In the other, was a Styrofoam cup of coffee. The aroma was strong. He probably liked it caffeinated. He fit the persona of no sugar. He was an adrenaline junkie. Growing up in the industry, Nova knew instinctively what Callan Duncan was. A gambler.

"I doubt you will see us ever again, Mr. Duncan. Both my dad and I appreciate your concern, but as you can see, I am fine, and my dad is fine."

"Oh, Miss Cross, I can see more than you give me credit for, but I will accept your excuse, no matter how lame it may be."

Nova opened her mouth to respond. Before she could utter her defiant response, Callan placed his finger gently across her lips. "Breathe. No need to give me your thoughts on my kindness."

Who the hell was this man? In the time that she and her father had arrived at the restaurant parking lot, where had he been? Where had he come from? Better yet, why wouldn't he disappear?

Nova was ready to end the conversation. She noticed that he reached and placed his hand on the necklace. He seemed nervous. Nova watched as Callan fidgeted with the items that were attached to the chain.

Callan did not want to bring attention to himself. He could not help it. When Callan was uncomfortable and needed reassurance, he would place his hand over the items and rub each one. Each held a significant memory. Was it a habit? More than likely, but one he could not give up. There were only a certain few he had shared the importance of the medallion and the three coins. This information had only been shared with a select few friends. They were not just acquaintances in the industry, but friends who knew Callan's background and his upbringing. Callan had made a promise. One that he intended to keep until his last dying breath.

Callan recalled how his grandfather and father had kept certain momentos in their pant pocket. Callan had been afraid that he would lose the precious items he had been given. They were pieces of love. Callan could not take a gamble on losing love.

Callan could tell by the narrowing of her eyes; Nova Cross was ready to plant him on the gravel. Before she could respond, Callan turned and began for the second time the trip to the entrance of the gates.

Nova's father looked at his daughter. Nova had just met her match. He knew what the young man was. It was him at that age. The age where you never thought about time. The age where you were invincible. The age where you could never make mistakes. The prime age of a gambler. Murray Cross knew, that even though Nova stated it with such conviction, they would be seeing Callan Duncan again. And it would be sooner than later.

CHAPTER 3

Nova knew she should never have turned around to watch him walk away. But she did. And so did he. Callan felt the stare. He did not need to second guess his instinct. He was close to entering the gates to begin his day. Something about the scenario he just left was not sitting well with him. He did not care. He turned and tilted his head.

Their eyes met. Nova had not moved. She was in the same spot that Callan had left her and her father. Before Nova could think any more about him and how to respond to his stare, Nova's father cleared his throat. "Staring ain't polite, baby girl. And let me tell you, the only reason men stare at a woman, so boldly, as he is doing, is because they want something. Nova, he is not staring just to stare. That young man wants something. And you ain't giving it to him. He has danger written all across him. Today you are not his something. Come on, Nova. It's time to get inside and ready for our day to begin. I can feel it. "It's gonna be a good day for our Betty Boots," Murray winked at his only child.

Looking at the backside of Callan Duncan, Nova acknowledged her father was right. At least for today, he was. She was not offering anything to anyone, no matter how sexy he looked or appeared to be. Tomorrow was another day to consider. Nova watched as he entered the admission gates.

Nova could only wonder why she was feeling unsettled. Before she could ponder any logical solution, Callan Duncan was gone.

Without missing a beat, Murray, as he had done since Nova was tiny, reached for her hand. The slightest of gestures, but it had become a routine that was more for Murray's piece of mind when keeping tabs on his daughter. Whether for her safety or just because, Nova anticipated and expected the security of her father's hand envelope hers.

Walking towards his seat and through the tunnel, Callan shook the hand of the regulars and answered all the questions: "How are you? Ready for the day? Have any favorites that you would like to share with us? Any secrets that you want to unveil?"

Callan loved this walk. It was the same walk he had done with his grandfather and father. They were the same questions. Funny how they had never changed. Old habits die hard and so it seemed with these questions. Stopping to see the scene before him, Callan knew without a doubt, this was God's artistry. It was where the heightened sense of destiny could arise, or the failure of defeat would lay down its ugly head. This was what Callan Duncan had been molded into. Just like his grandfather and father, a gambler.

As Callan sat down in his box, he could hear the sound of the chairs being opened, the program book pages being thumbed through, and then a quiet sigh of being done. The first race of the day was about to begin.

Even if you were not a race fan or could not comprehend the race program, there was no denying the exhilaration of watching these majestic creatures begin their lineup. Callan stood up. He placed his hands on the rail in front of him and gripped as tight as he could. He had learned this stance from his grandfather. No matter if a win or a loss, the rails would hold you on both outcomes.

But Callan was not standing because of need, Nova Cross and her father, Murray Cross, were making their way through the seats to be placed a few rows below Callan.

Callan watched as his daughter did a quick perusal of the box and then whispered to her father. He kissed her on the side of cheek and nodded in the direction of Callan.

Nova questioned her dad as they found their box. She needed to get something to drink. If he were going to bet, she asked that he wait until she returned. He kissed her on the side of the cheek and winked. "I cannot guarantee I can wait to place a bet, but if I'm not here, then you know where I'll be."

Nova stepped into the aisle. She was not thinking about the excuse she had just told her father. Her only thought was should she walk past him? She shook her head. Stop it, she told herself. He was like everyone else attending the track. He was a gambler. She had met plenty of guys like him. She had fallen for a few like him. Nova had also learned the hard way about falling for a gambler. Everyday life was a chance. Whether that chance became risky or not, was placed on the odds of the choices made. This life had chosen her. Nova had not chosen it. Her path had been pre-determined, not by her choice, but by custom of an old habit that had been long-established by three generations.

Callan could not help but notice when she rose. He watched her father gently kiss her on the cheek. She more than likely was going to place a bet for the first race of the day. She was walking in his direction. She stopped and turned around to look back at her father. Her eyes then looked at Callan. Callan's eyes locked with Nova's. She did not flinch from his stare. Callan wanted to know more than the obvious. What was her story?

Nova was frozen. She could not help but admire his physique, but her thoughts returned again to his selection of wardrobe for the track. The words her father stated rang through her mind. "He is dangerous, Nova. Steer clear." Callan was dangerous. Her nervousness in walking past him was not her concern. It was the fact she had purposefully made the decision to do so.

Nova took the first step. Before she could even walk past Callan's section, he stepped out to meet her. "Going my way?" Nova smiled. "No, you happen to be going my way." Callan grinned. At least her response was cheeky.

Good. Maybe she wanted to play. "Well, then how about I walk with you just in case you need protection?"

"It's Callan, correct?"

Callan winked. "It is. I did not know if you would remember or not. I must have made a good impression."

Nova knew what he was doing. So similar to so many lines she had heard when a man was beginning the "flirting" conversation. "First, please let me assure you, I can take care of myself. I do not need your protection. Second, Callan Duncan, I know what you are doing. Feel free to give it your best shot, but I can guarantee you, I seen and heard it all. You cannot impress me. You will be gone in less than 24 hours. You, Mr. Duncan, are just a small bump in my day today. Just like a bump on a pickle. Nothing more. Nothing less. You barely even know the bump is there unless you accidentally rub your hand across it."

"Ouch. I've never been compared to a bump nor a pickle. This is a first for me," Callan laughed.

Nova laughed. "I'm pretty sure I can come up with a few more comparisons. But I'll play nice today. My daddy always told me first impressions are lasting impressions, and, of course, make the biggest impressions. So, if you find it necessary that I need protection by all means walk with me. If I'm not back in a few, my father will come looking for me. Finding me with you, is not going to make a good impression on my father."

Callan could not argue with her. He did not want to argue with her. But he was not ready to finish the conversation. He was enjoying the underlying meaning to the words being used. Callan knew when sexual tension was in the air with a woman. And it was so with Nova Cross. His senses were heightened to her closeness to him. Her perfume scent was a small whisper of jasmine that he had captured while she was standing near him.

"Well, I do not want to get on the bad side of your father. I rather like him," Callan stated. Before Nova could respond how did he know if her father liked him, Callan placed his hand on the small of her back and led her forward.

His touch sent a shiver through her. Nova had forgotten what that "feeling" felt like. The first touch. His touch.

Lost in her emotions, Nova did not hear any of what Callan had been asking. 'I'm sorry, Callan. I was lost in my thoughts for the day and how Betty Boots would do. Ask me again."

"I was inquiring if you were like me. A generation raised around horses and the thrill of the race?"

Nova smiled. "Yes, I am just like you. From the time I began walking, I was right beside my father. I learned to read because of the program book. I learned to do math because of betting. And yes, I never had close friends because of this industry and always wanting to please my father."

"Well, then, we have something in common. Pretty sure, you didn't think that was going to happen this morning when you stated with such conviction, you would not see me again. I hate to point the obvious out, but we are a match made in heaven," Callan laughed.

Nova did not want him to see how much this affected her at this moment. She could not help but shake her head and smile. "Callan, whether we are match in heaven or hell, is yet to be determined. But I do know one thing for sure, I am thirsty. My dad is going to be worried, and more than likely, we are going to miss placing our bets for the first race. As you know, that is a big no no. The old superstition is going to rear its ugly head and then I'll have to listen to my father tell me the story of this superstition and its importance. Let's get our orders, return to our seats, place our bets and if you are still around, with enough money in your pocket from the day, I'll see how the bump on the pickle is looking."

Callan put his hand out. "Deal. Let's shake on it."

And with such intent, Callan reached for Nova's hand. Except, he did not shake her hand. Callan entwined his hand into hers and brought it to his chest. "Oh, I plan on being more than a bump on a pickle with you, Nova Cross."

CHAPTER 4

Nova could not get the word out of her mind. When he had intertwined his hand through hers, Nova saw it. It was in cursive. It was one word. It was the word "Lucky". And from where the tattoo had been placed, it was there for a specific reason.

Nova could not think about the reason why. Her only thoughts were of the day. Lady luck had not been good to her father or Betty Boots. Even though Betty Boots had come in third, it was still not enough to show justification for earnings made.

It was time to pack it up and call it a day. Nova squeezed her father's arm. "Tomorrow is another day, another chance. She will run better tomorrow. I know it."

Murray Cross heard his daughter's words. What he couldn't tell her was that tomorrow was today. They needed the win today. Reaching for her hand just as he did at the restaurant, they began to walk to the backside. The routine was always the same. Both Murray and Nova would head to the backside. On the way, they would speak with a few of the trainers and the owners and get their insight into the day's races. Finally, they would stand in front of Betty Boots' stall and check on her. More than likely, Betty Boots was fine but seeing is believing.

As they made their way into the barn and to Betty Boots' stall, Nova felt the hair stand up on her arms. Something was wrong. Her father placed his arm out to stop her. "Listen to me, Nova. No matter what, no matter what happens in these next few minutes, if questioned, you did not know anything. Do you hear me? Do you understand?"

Nova felt her heart begin to beat rapidly. What had her father done? It was not who was standing in front of Betty Boots' stall, but why was he standing there. There was not just one, but two men standing to the side of the stall, just close enough to the man that Nova had seen first, like a bodyguard stance. Nova felt as if she were in a movie, and she knew what the outcome was about to be.

"Remember, Nova. Remember what I told you." And with a small push on Nova's waist, her father had placed her behind him.

The man did not move. He waited until Nova's father was in earshot. "Murray, or should I address you with more professionalism since your daughter is with you?"

Nova watched her father's shoulder's tense. "You may call me whatever you want. You just need to tell me why you are here. I thought we had an understanding that nothing would take place until after the outcome of tomorrow's race."

The man, who her father had still not called his name, cleared his throat. "To be honest, I am a bit unsure if she can pull off a win. But no matter, the understanding still stands as you state. Nothing will take place until after tomorrow's race. I just wanted reassurance that we were all in agreement. I assume nothing has changed to cancel the agreement?"

Nova watched as her father shook his head no. Then she heard the words that would change her life forever. "Mr. Windsor, please let me explain that my daughter, Nova, is to be kept safe. There will be no harm to come to her. You made this promise to me."

"Mr. Cross, I can promise that no harm will come to your beautiful daughter. I assume you are speaking about the pretty lady that is standing behind you? As for harm to anyone else, there is no guarantee. As you stated, we must wait for the outcome tomorrow."

Nova could not breathe. She was getting light-headed. She was going to pass out from the words of Mr. Windsor. Nova realized that her father was involved in something much larger than just a race. She reached to place her hand on the barn, and that's when it happened.

She felt something strong catch her and then she heard his voice. "Mr. Cross, I was just shooting the shit with several of the trainers and going over the races tomorrow, when I noticed you and Nova may need some company. Is everything okay?"

Nova looked up into the sky. Her prayers had not been answered, but at least a miracle had appeared out of nowhere in the form of Callan Duncan.

Without forethought to what implications he would suffer after, Callan turned Nova around. He leaned in and kissed Nova. She did not pull back. He kissed her slowly with hopes that the new-found acquaintances would get Callan's drift. "Sweetheart, if Betty is okay, we need to get back to the hotel and eat a little something and turn in. It's been a big day. I need you and Pops both rested. What do you say we call it a night?"

"Gentlemen, I hate to cut the conversation short, but I'm sure you understand the importance of not just all of us, but even Betty Boots getting some much-needed rest. If you will excuse us, we will be on our way. I'm sure we will see you tomorrow."

Nova nodded. "I am a bit frazzled from the day's events, Callan. Daddy, are you ready to turn in?" Nova reached from behind her father and squeezed his hand reassuringly.

Murray looked at his daughter and then at Callan Duncan. "I am, sugar. Callan, you are correct. Everything and everyone are as it should be for tonight. Tomorrow is another day. The obstacles will still be there."

Callan nodded. "Gentlemen, thank you. We shall see you in the morning. Sleep tight."

CHAPTER 5

Eternity was considered forever. Silence was meant to be broken. So far, it seemed eternity was in front of him. Callan was unsure of how to broach Nova and Mr. Cross. He was unsure of what had just transpired.

Exiting through the same gates they entered, Callan gave the lead to Nova and her father. Before Callan could inquire, Murray turned and commented, "I owe you an explanation, Mr. Duncan."

"Stop, Mr. Cross. It's Callan. I do not need an explanation. It is none of my business. I'm just thankful I was here to get my kiss," Callan smiled.

Nova could not help but smile at the comment Callan made. Of all the things to say, that was not what she had expected after the encounter. She, herself, was unsure of what had just taken place. Other than the fact, her father had done something she was sure she needed to be made aware of.

Mr. Cross chuckled. He liked Callan. He was honest and he did not look like the typical trickster or gambler that Mr. Cross had known. There was something about the young man that was lost. He did not become upset nor bang his program book against the rails. He stood still, watched and then after each race, sat down and reviewed the program book. Callan Duncan kept his emotions in check. Mr. Cross knew there was something more to Callan than just being lucky. It was something that could not be learned. It was an innate ability to understand that there was no such thing as luck. It was a gift.

"Well, since you have received a kiss, the only matter left remaining would be dinner. Please let me treat you tonight as my way of saying thank you for being there at the right time?"

Callan knew he was sincere with his offer. Callan was hungry. He was not ready to leave the company of Mr. Cross. He did not want to admit that he also wanted to get to know his daughter a bit better.

"Thank you. I accept your invitation." Callan took a step closer to where Nova was standing. He looked into her eyes. "And, who knows, I might just get another free kiss."

Nova scoffed. "Think again, lover boy. You are not going to be that lucky. Your best bet is on the dinner."

Mr. Cross motioned for them both to come on. "There's more time for arguing while we are feeding our faces. Come on, before they close. Callan, you can follow us. I'm headed to The Backside Grill. Do you know the location?"

"I do, Mr. Cross. I frequented the restaurant many times with my grandfather and father after the races. I will meet you both there." Callan turned and walked towards his truck.

Opening the truck door and sliding into the seat, Nova looked at her father with one eyebrow up in the air. "Daddy, have you lost your mind? This is just as bad as the encounter with the men a few moments ago. We do not know Callan Duncan. We have no idea of his background. He could be part of something worse than the agreement you made reference to with those shysters. That's for a later discussion. Right now, I'm concerned about him."

Murray grinned. "Nova, put your seatbelt on. Stop worrying. My mind has changed since this morning. There is something special about him. My intuition tells me that Callan is honest and sincere in all that he does. My intuition also tells me he is a guarded man with his feelings and does not display emotion with ease."

"Daddy, fine. I get it. What I don't get is that conversation that just occurred. I do not understand all that took place with regards to the agreement, but I can only surmise, tomorrow is either a make it or break it kind of day for you, which means you and I, since we are a team?"

"Let's enjoy your dinner. Let's enjoy Callan's company. I will explain everything in the morning before we leave. Okay?"

Nova knew her father was skirting around disclosing any information to her. He was protecting her. There had only been several times that something of this nature had occurred. Nova knew her father had come out smelling like a rose on these few occasions. She did not feel that this was going to happen with these men. For the first time in her life, Nova was not worried. She was scared. She was frightened of what her father may have done. She was afraid of what might happen tomorrow if everything did not pan out as her father had planned. She was fearful for tomorrow.

Callan saw them pull into the parking lot. He walked towards their truck. He waited until Mr. Cross had turned the truck off. He reached to open Nova's door.

"You are incredible. You are really making one hell of an impression on my father. What are you doing, Callan? What's your motive?"

Callan smiled. "I know what I am doing, Nova. And I know the motive. It's you."

Callan knew he had caught her off guard. He watched her as she stepped from the truck. "Don't be too sure on that motive. You may have won my father over, but I'm nowhere near the finish line."

"Give me time, Nova. That's all I need or ask. Who knows you might get lucky."

Nova's mind went back to the words she had seen tatted on his hand, "Lucky". There was no such thing as luck or being lucky. Life was nothing but a gamble. Callan Duncan had met his match.

CHAPTER 6

Walking side by side with Mr. Cross and Nova, Callan enjoyed the small talk. The teasing back and forth between father and daughter was a comfort to Callan. Mr. Cross was inquiring if Callan had been happy with the days' races and their results. Callan smiled. "For the most part. There were not any major surprises." Nova shook her head. "Dad, I'm sure Callan does not want to talk shop."

"I don't mind, Nova. It's all I know. It's all I was raised on. Other than trying to appear normal while attending school, I attended more races than school days."

"You're joking, right," Nova exclaimed.

As they approached the entrance of the restaurant, Callan reached for the door. He opened it and made sure that Mr. Cross and Nova were inside. Nova turned before Callan could stop in mid stride.

Nova bumped into Callan. She looked up at Callan. "You might be able to impress my father with your knowledge of the industry, but not me. I've seen your kind before. The track is your life. The horses are your love. The wins are never enough."

"Nova, you have no idea who I am. You are making a lot of assumptions based on one day. Let me reassure you, there is more underneath this suit. Much more. The only question is are you ready to undo the first button and reveal what is hidden?"

Nova knew he was playing with her. She was quite sure by the tone of his voice and the whisper, which he had relayed the challenge, he was not teasing Nova. He was making a promise.

Callan observed Nova. He knew she did not know what to make of him. Callan remembered a saying that his father had shared with him in his teen years. "Keep 'em guessing, son. If you don't challenge them, then the interest wanes and they'll look somewhere else for that emotional high." He was right. Callan loved a challenge, and he could sense Nova was a challenge.

"Don't worry, Nova. I promise tonight will just be small talk. No need to make any major decisions that may alter your life. Just good food and good conversation. There will not be a quiz this evening. Relax."

Nova laughed. "Don't make promises you cannot keep, Mr. Duncan." Nova did not want Callan to know how nervous she was. It was not because of Callan and his closeness to her or his scent of masculinity. It was not because when she bumped into Callan, she had felt how hard his chest was. It was not because of his deep blue eyes that looked as inviting as the ocean. Callan Duncan had left an impression on Nova. She prayed her father would not reveal in their conversation the trouble that she and her father were truly in. Nova did not know why, but she did not need Callan's sympathy nor his concern. She would be able to handle the situation just as she had done so many times before. Tomorrow would bring a new day and bring a new race for Betty Boots. Nova was confident that their troubles would disappear tomorrow and so would Callan Duncan.

As the waitress checked one last time at their table to see if anything else was needed, she laid the ticket on the table. "You are more than welcome to pay me or pay at the front. I hope you all had a wonderful evening and return."

Nova went to reach for the tab. She did not like it when others paid for her and her father's meals. It made Nova feel that she needed to do something to repay them for their act of kindness. She definitely did not need this burden placed on her with repaying Callan Duncan. She was pretty confident. He would not accept cash but instead would request an alternative payment.

As she did, he placed his hand over hers. "Nova, stop. I insist. This is my treat. I enjoyed myself this evening with both you and your father. It was nice to just talk of everything and of nothing, if that makes sense to you." Nova could not move her hand. She could not remember one word he had just said. Her brain shut off at the word "treat". Nova imagined the types of treats that Callan was used to. She was not going to be one of them. "Callan, we can pay for our meal. There is no need to feel obligated to pay. Dad and I are fine."

Callan nodded. "How about the next meal, you get? Let's consider this an introductory meal to new beginnings and newfound friends." Callan began to rub her hand. "If you do not agree with me, I am not going to remove my hand. I rather like the softness of your skin between my fingers."

Okay. Now he was teasing her. Nova stared at him. Her father was busy talking to the waitress. Nova tried to remove her hand. Callan would not release it. "I know what you are doing, and it is not going to work. I know your kind, Callan. All the pleasantries of being a gentleman and looking very debonair, but in reality, you are a wolf in sheep's clothing or in your case, a suit. Just because you feel that my dad and I need rescuing, we don't. We were fine before you came along, and we will be fine once you are gone. Guys, like you, don't hang around very long. Commitment is too difficult for you. Let's call it a night. Since you feel so strongly about paying for our meals, I'll say thank you. If we see you tomorrow, that's great. If we don't, it's no big deal."

Callan knew what she was doing. Nova was throwing the word "commitment" at him, when Callan knew she was right there with him. It just wasn't Callan. It was Nova Cross who was afraid of commitment.

Callan watched to make sure that Mr. Cross and Nova made it to their vehicle. As they pulled out, Callan walked to his truck. He did not have a good feeling about tomorrow for Nova. There had been no discussion at the table tonight. Callan had watched the exchange between father and daughter. He sensed that Nova had cautioned her father not to mention the industry but to keep it to small talk. Nova did just that. Callan started the truck and began the thoughts of what they were hiding, were they being honest with him, and finally, what was so important about the outcome of tomorrow.

Before Callan realized it, instinct made the turn into his driveway. He turned the truck off. Whatever his thoughts were, the answers would be revealed tomorrow. Unlocking the door, Callan walked in and stopped in the entry way. He was not known to eat lunch with the industry people. His father had always told him to keep his distance. Callan heard the words his father preached: "When you get too close to someone, this is when you begin to care. Caring can be a disappointment. Guard your heart." Callan knew it was too late. He had already begun to care about Nova Cross. He wanted to protect her. Whatever trouble Nova and her father were in, there was always a way out. It might be ugly, but there was always a solution to the problem.

For tonight though, Callan needed to do one last minute review of the program's races for tomorrow. The fifth race caught his eye. This was the race that Mr. Cross and Nova's horse was listed. He checked the other competitors. It would be a nice race. All had level playing field to win. Odds were pretty good. Laying the program down, Callan walked through his home. This home had been in his family for three generations. A rule of thumb with his grandfather and father was that under no circumstances was the house ever gambled or put up for stakes as a debt. Callan had kept that promise.

CHAPTER 7

The alarm went off. Callan did not waste any time. There was no time to hit the snooze button. Callan wanted to arrive at the restaurant before Nova and her father. He assumed they would be there just like yesterday. Again, old habits were hard to change.

Looking through his closet, Callan picked his favorite suit. He had more than one of the same exact suits. He didn't consider it "the lucky suit". It was his memories of how his grandfather and father dressed. Was it superstition or was it routine? Callan had no need to analyze. It was both. The superstition of black and white. The routine that was peaceful and calming.

Callan did not need to question anyone about his wardrobe. He did not need to ask for approval before leaving his home. He did not need to turn around to second guess himself. Locking the front door, Callan gripped the door. He felt it in the air. He knew it. Today would determine a new direction.

Leaving the hotel before the sun rose had become the norm when they were on the road with Betty Boots. Travelling from track to track and race to race, Nova knew Betty Boots would expect her special treat. This was an essential piece of Betty's day. Sitting in the truck, Nova had already pulled her seatbelt and locked it. She knew her father was going over the checklist in his head. She also knew that he was worried.

When they returned to the hotel, Nova could not hear her father's footsteps. Typically, he would turn the television on, and she could hear his movements but tonight, there was nothing. Nova was worried because she knew her father was worried. Nova could not help it.

She watched her father walk towards the truck. A tear slid down her cheek. He was her everything. Nova had a purpose with her father. She had direction with her father. Today would be okay. They had been in pickles like this before in the industry.

Nova could not think about what may happen. Her thoughts had turned to him. She had thought about him all night. She laid her head down and dreamt about him. She woke up to the emotion of excitement, not for the race, but for expectation.

Nova winked at her father as he backed out of the hotel parking lot. "We got this daddy. It's going to be a beautiful day. You know Betty is waiting. She's probably getting a bit impatient. You know we arrive while it's still a bit dark. We need her to be relaxed, even though we may not be."

"Now what makes you think I am not relaxed, honey? We have nothing to worry about. Betty only needs to win, place or show. She has finished with all three. I personally feel I am much more relaxed than you. I can tell your thoughts are elsewhere, too. Are you wondering if he will attend today's race? Are you wondering if you will see him?"

"Dad, lord no! Yesterday was a one-time meeting. I doubt he has given any more thought to us. He has his own personal agenda. Like you said, he is a gambler. You have told me more than once that love does not exist with a gambler. Are you changing your mind since meeting Callan Duncan?"

Murray Cross knew what his daughter was up to. She wanted him to admit what she had been thinking. Callan Duncan may be worth the risk.

Murray Cross looked over at his daughter. More than life itself, he loved his one and only child. He had made mistakes. He knew that his last mistake may catch up to him if all did not go as planned. "Nova, I am not going to say anything bad about the young man. I like him. He did not try to impress us last night with losses and wins. He was genuine in his conversation." Murray knew without a doubt, today's race would determine a new direction. He could only pray that it would be good for both he and Nova.

Before the sun could even make its mark through the windows, the restaurant was packed. Callan was not the only one who kept in line with superstition. He opened the doors to the restaurant where the regulars would be hanging out waiting to see who visited "their" restaurant. Callan smiled. Most of the regulars were reviewing the races for the day. Callan inhaled. This was what he loved. The smell of the smoke of the grill. The sound of the toaster popping. The aroma of coffee.

The good morning handshakes. But the best part was the most familiar part. "Good morning, honey. Still the same?"

"Allie, how long have you been asking me this question?" Allie chuckled. "Since you could walk, Callan. But it never hurts to ask. I keep thinking one day you might just surprise me."

Callan hugged her. "I can't. They never did. I can't break tradition. So, yes, the same as always."

Allie kissed Callan on the side of his cheek as she had done for most of his life. "I know. I miss both of them. I'll put your order in. Be right back with you."

This was Callan's life. Allie, Jimmy and the restaurant. This was where he belonged. Callan reached for them. He placed his hand over each. Just confirmation they were still around his neck.

Opening the doors, Nova watched the exchange between the owner and Callan. Nova could tell that there was something special between the two.

Nova felt her father squeeze her hand. "If you keep staring, folk are going to put two and two together. Best move over to an empty table. And, if sees you watching him, Nova, he will think the same."

Nova turned. "And what's that, daddy?"

Murray laughed. "You're staring just a bit too long. We have not even been seated. If it's obvious to me, it's obvious to others, and especially to him should he catch you."

Nova tilted her head. She was ready to give her father

a snarky comment and then it happened. Just as yesterday, Callan Duncan reached for the middle of his chest. Nova watched as his hand gently rubbed the necklace. Nova's eyes were drawn to his chest, again. What was wrong with her? Before she could look away, he was walking towards her.

The restaurant doors opened. Callan felt her presence. How long had she been watching him? Callan looked at her. She was breathtaking. The best part was Callan knew she had no idea of her natural beauty. Her hair was the color of the sun rising in the morning. It wasn't red, but a light ginger. Wispy layered pieces framed her face. Her bangs were straight. Callan did not know how old she was. He assumed she was probably close to his age.

Walking towards her, Callan observed her inhale. As she did, her breasts rose in time with her breathing. Callan hated to admit it, but he was glad that Nova and her father had returned. "Hello, again, Nova. I trust that you slept well and ready to hit the ground running or racing."

Just like yesterday, Nova could not help but notice he was dressed in the same attire. "Good morning, Callan. We just finished checking on Betty and dad wanted some coffee before the gates opened."

Mr. Cross reached his out to shake Callan's. "Good morning, Callan. My daughter is not telling the truth. I did want coffee, but Nova also needed something from the restaurant. And she found it."

Callan could not help it. "Nova, what were you looking

for?"

Nova bit her lower lip. She knew Callan was teasing her. She also knew her father was watching the exchange between her and Callan.

Before Nova could respond, her father inquired if Callan would like to sit with them and review the races for the day. "Yes sir. I'll share my insight if you do the same." Murray nodded. He liked this young man.

Without any word of caution or are you ready, Nova felt Callan's hand on the small of her back. He leaned in and whispered, "Is the booth in the corner, okay?"

A shiver went through Nova. Callan felt her response to his closeness. Without forethought to how she would react, Callan leaned in again. "I'm glad you returned."

Nova lost her voice. She couldn't talk. Hell, she couldn't move to the booth in the corner. Nova turned into Callan. His open shirt was her undoing. His scent was of musk. It was not strong. It was just enough that she would remember it.

What possessed her to reach for his necklace, she had no idea. She placed her finger on the coin. As she touched the coin, it slid to the side to reveal another coin. Nova looked up at Callan. "They are special to you?"

"Yes, very. I will tell you one day what they mean to me. Let's get you to that corner booth, Nova. The races will be starting. If your father is like most, he does not like to be late to anything."

Nova nodded. The day had begun with uncertainty. Nova

did not know why, but the words "I will tell you one day" held promise for Nova. Sliding into the booth with her father, Nova leaned onto her father's shoulders. Everything was going to be okay.

CHAPTER 8

Callan could not help but be concerned. He was doing fine with the races. He was ahead of the game. But she was not. Callan watched as Nova placed her head on the banister. Her father placed his hand on her back as if in comfort. Callan knew that the next race would be the one that Nova and her father's horse, Betty Boots, would be running.

Just by the actions portrayed by Murray Cross, Callan surmised they were in financial trouble.

Even though they walked from the restaurant to the track together, the mood was somber. Callan allowed Nova and her father to walk through first. Callan had been stopped by several regulars requesting his advice. When Nova turned around, he nodded. She returned his nod and kept walking. Callan knew she would continue without him. After shaking hands and speaking the industry, Callan was in his box. Nova and Murray were in theirs.

Callan noticed that the regulars were not even excited about the wins. There had been no rain or fog that morning. The track was fast. The finishes were tight. There should have been excitement taking place and yet, the crowd was subdued. Callan looked around. He felt it. Tension was in the air.

Nova watched as Betty Boots was placed in the trailer. There were seven horses running this race. If Betty finished in the top three, all would be well. Nova watched as Jerry, their jockey, walked Betty Boots into the fourth shoot. Nova reached for her dad's hand. Without missing a beat, he squeezed Nova's hand. Murray could not look at his daughter. He could not tell Nova how deep he was in. Just one more win. That's all Murray needed. One more win.

The call was made. And the shoots opened. Betty Boots was doing well. Coming around the bend, she was in the top five. Callan could not help but watch Nova and her father's reactions. By the way, Murray was waving the program in the air, Callan knew there was more to this race. Callan had to be near her. He left his box and walked towards Nova. He needed to be close.

Nova was nervous. Betty Boots was holding tight. She had not gone ahead in the pack. Still in the top five, she had that round to come off of. Nova could not breathe. She was holding her breath. Her father was squeezing her hand tighter and tighter as Betty Boots got closer to the finish line. Nova knew he was there. She did not need to turn. Why she did what she did, she had no idea. Nova slowly moved her hand down her right side.

Callan moved closer. He stood beside Nova. He slid his hand next to hers. Would she accept his gesture? Before he could move any closer, Nova entwined her hand with his. Callan kept his focus on the race. He asked out of ear shot of her father. "Nova, I know something is going on. You do not have to tell me. Just know, I am here."

Nova did not know how to respond. She was afraid to look at him. She knew she would burst into tears. She was so tired of worrying about the next day, the next race, and the next dilemma her father would place them in. "Thank you, Callan."

Callan knew just by the placement of the horses, Betty Boots was not going to finish in the top three. The pack was too tight, and her jockey could not position himself to get past the other horses. Callan watched Mr. Cross. He knew it, as well. Callan looked at Nova. A tear had trickled down her cheek. Callan turned to Nova. "Remember, what I said, Nova."

The announcer called the winner, the second, and the third place finishers. Betty Boots finished fourth. Murray turned to his daughter. "Nova, we need to get down to the barns and get Betty packed for the trip back home. We must leave now."

Callan stepped back to allow Nova to let go of his hand. Nova did not look back. She reached for her father's hand as always. As they began their walk back into the tunnel, Callan remained still. He stared out into the distance. He had never encountered someone like Nova. He did not know her and yet, he did. She was him. She had been raised travelling late into the night and rising before the sun came up. Sometimes you were afforded the opportunity to eat and rest and at other times, you did have the funds for the special eccentricities..

Callan could not let her go. Callan knew their paths were meant to cross. Looking up into the sky, Callan winked. "I know, dad. I know. Love is a gamble."

CHAPTER 9

Murray Cross knew he needed to tell Nova sooner than later what he had done. There was never a good time to share bad news. He was about to tell Nova when they appeared from out of nowhere.

Murray let go of his daughter's hand. "Nova, listen to me. Don't look at me. Keep walking with me. No matter what happens, no matter what happens to me, high tail it to Betty's stall. Take her away. Walk as far as you can, until your walk takes me from your sight."

"Daddy, what have you done?"

Before Murray could answer, the two men looked at Nova. "Well, Mr. Cross, you didn't tell us you had this lucky little charm as part of the package."

Murray pushed Nova to the side. "She's not part of the deal. She never was."

Nova kissed her father on the side of the cheek. She stated with a clear voice for the two men to hear, "I'll go take care of business. I'll see you in a few, daddy."

Nova did not give the men time to say anything further. She took a left. Her father knew this was not the way to Betty Boots' stall. He couldn't worry about what she was doing. He needed to satisfy a bet. A bet that he could not repay. Murray knew these men would not take no for an answer. He knew things were about to go south.

Nova knew her father saw the turn she had taken. It was nowhere near Betty's stall. Hopefully, Nova could find him. After all, he did tell her that he would be there. If she were Callan Duncan, where would he go before heading home?

Trying to keep one eye on her father and one ear to the ground, Nova was not paying attention to where she was walking. Before she realized what had happened, two hands reached out to stop her. "Whoa, Nova. Where are you going?"

Nova did not mean to, but it just happened. She laid her head against his chest. "Callan, I need you."

Callan felt a sense of dread. "Nova, what's going on? Are you okay? Is Murray, okay? Look at me, where is your father?"

Nova hated this. She hated it when she had no control over the tears. She did not like to cry. A cry was not just a verb, it was an emotion. "He needs your help, Callan. Daddy needs you. Can you help us?"

Can you help us was a standard question in the industry. It was more common than most people realized. "Nova, I'm here. Take me to your father. Where is he?"

He reached for Nova's hand and entwined his fingers through hers. "It's going to be fine. Trust me." Nova nodded in agreement.

As Nova and Callan turned the corner to the barn, Callan could hear their loud voices. Picking up the pace, Nova whispered, "Callan, he lost a bet. He owes them money."

"Don't worry. I've seen them before. We got this. Look at me, Nova. I need to know you are safe and away from harm. I want you to wait over here. Let me handle this. Yes?"

"I understand. Please help daddy."

Callan stepped in front of her. He placed his hands on her arms and pulled her close to his chest. Callan kissed her as if they were in a scene at the airport. Callan was leaving. Nova was walking away. He placed his hand on the side of her face. "Stay put, please. Don't reveal yourself."

Nova inhaled. She looked at this man. Nova knew without a doubt, her daddy needed Callan. "I will. I promise, Callan."

Callan started walking towards Murray and the two men. Callan cleared his throat to capture them off guard. "Mr. Cross, is there anything I can help with or is the matter under control?"

Murray acknowledged Callan. The two gentlemen eyed Callan up and down. Callan could sense they were going to say something until Callan placed his hand in the air. "Guys, I think we are done here. Mr. Cross and I have other obligations that must be tended to. I am sure that whatever you have requested from Mr. Cross will be handled in a timely professional manner. Murray, we need to go ahead and get her taken care of. We don't have a lot of time before we head out."

Callan knew they were sizing him up to see whether it was worth the risk. The two men made a move closer to Murray when out of the dark, she appeared. All heads turned to her. Why, why had she not listened? She was putting herself in danger. This should have been a warning for Callan. Her stubbornness to disobey him only made him desire her more.

"Gentlemen, I assume Murray has both your cell numbers so we can follow up with you regarding this meeting?" Both shook their heads. "Good, I'll be in touch, not Mr. Cross, do I make myself clear?" Callan could tell by their non-chalant attitudes, that they didn't care about Mr. Cross. At the moment, their attention was drawn to the beautiful woman walking towards them. Callan guided Murray towards him.

"I will be in touch tomorrow, gentlemen," Nova stated.

The men copied each other with their words, "You better or else. The older man stated firmly: "We will do what is necessary to obtain what is owed to us. You understand what we are saying?"

"Yes, every word," Callan stated. Callan had Murray far enough way that if they came after Murray, Callan would be able to step in between and protect Murray.

As she drew closer to her father and Callan, Nova knew he was pissed. She began to offer an explanation. "Nova Cross, I will deal with you later. Let's get Betty Boots taken care of. It will only take a few minutes at her barn stall. And then, I'll deal with you not being able to follow instructions."

Murray could not help it. "She didn't listen to you either?"

Callan winked. "Nope. I knew she wouldn't."

"Good, so long as you are not disappointed, Callan," Murray laughed.

"Enough both of you. You cannot tag team me. And if I hadn't walked around the barn when I did, who knows what might have happened to both of you," Nova stated with conviction.

Callan stopped midstride and turned. He placed his hand under her chin. Again, Callan could not resist. He kissed Nova

Cross. He kissed her hard. He kissed her long. Callan pulled away. "Like I said, Miss Cross, we will deal with you not being able to follow instructions, later."

Murray chuckled. He liked Callan Duncan. He may have misjudged Callan Duncan. Murray watched as both Nova and Callan approached Betty's stall. Murray stood still and observed Betty. Betty Boots had a special bond with Nova. Murray saw Callan walk closer and place his hand on Betty Boots. She nuzzled her head into Callan's shoulder. The night routine was always the same with Betty. Murray could hear both Callan and Nova speaking in hushed tones to Betty. As Nova said goodbye to Betty for the night, Callan remained close.

Murray tilted his head. Maybe he wasn't so bad after all. Maybe Callan Ducan would break the mold of the industry. Just maybe, Murray Cross had misjudged Callan Duncan, and he was not the scoundrel Murray had assumed.

CHAPTER 10

Nova was trying to walk as slowly as possible. She was hoping to give Callan time to forgive her. Walking towards the parking lot, Callan was right beside her. Step for step, stride for stride. "You're only delaying the inevitable, Nova. Don't make me put you over my shoulder and carry you the rest of the way to the truck."

"Fine, go ahead and give it to me but I protected you and dad. Those two men were going to do something horrible to my father and to you, as well, had I not stepped out from the shadows, who knows what would have happened. I saved you from getting the lights beat out of you."

"Seriously. You saved me? You're going to take this stance. Nova Cross, you have no idea what seeing you walking from the shadows did to me. You thought you would distract them; I know. But all you did, baby, was distract me. I was worried what would happen to you."

Murray was listening to the bantering back and forth. He felt light-headed. He had been ahead of Callan and Nova. He turned and looked at each of them. "Nova, sweetheart, he has a point. Let's get back...."

Murray Cross did not finish the sentence. He crumpled to the ground. Nova screamed. "Daddy!" Rushing to Murray, Callan placed his hands under Murray's arms to pull him up.

Before Callan could ask if he was okay, Murray looked at him. "Callan, I'm still breathing. I'm just tired. I just need to get some rest."

Callan smiled. He knew where Nova got her stubbornness from. It was honest. "Yes, you do, and I know exactly where you will be resting."

"Nova, I'm going to walk your father to my truck. You both are coming home with me. We will get your luggage and anything else from the hotel tomorrow. Tonight, though, I need to get some rest and the only way to do that is take you both home with me."

"Callan. No. I can take care of my father. We do not need your help."

Callan grinned. "Nova, I didn't hear me offer you a choice. There is no choice. You can follow me in your dad's truck. It's not that far from here. I'll drive slowly. But neither you nor Murray are leaving my sight. Again, it's not up for discussion."

Nova did not want to know how much her having no choice in the matter made it easier for her not to worry about her father and the possibility of those two men knowing their hotel or their whereabouts. Nova needed to sort all that had transpired tonight so she could make plans for Betty Boots and what was to occur regarding the next race.

"Fine, but I want you to know I am protesting this entire idea," Nova stated with conviction.

"Yeah, yeah. Protest. Conviction. Go get in the truck and pull over here and let's get your father to my home so he can rest, and we can, too."

Pulling into the driveway, Nova was shocked. She did not know what she expected, but it was not this. It was a long driveway that she followed Callan. She thought they would never get to Callan's home when she saw it. It was a log cabin. It had a wraparound porch. The landscaping lights illuminated the beautiful home. Who was Callan Duncan?

Callan placed the truck in park. He looked over at Murray who was sound asleep. His head leaning on the window. He looked from the rear-view mirror as she parked the truck. She was walking towards him. He opened the door. "Nova, your dad fell asleep. I'll wake him. Here are the keys to unlock the front door. The light inside is censored and will come on automatically. Keep the door open for us, please."

"I understand, Callan. Thank you." Nova heard Callan wake Murray up with the words "Mr. Cross, we are home. Come on. I'll help you."

Callan and her dad were not far behind her. Nova held the door open as Callan was holding her dad around his waist to make sure he did not fall. Walking in, Callan led Murray to the spare bedroom. This had been Callan's room growing up. Callan sensed her behind him. He sat Murray on the side of the bed. Nova came around and began to take his boots off.

Nova turned to Callan. "Don't worry about his shirt or pants, Callan. We've slept in our clothes plenty of times in order to be ready for early morning travels."

Callan could not help but stare as he watched Nova place the blanket over her father. She kissed him on the forehead.

Callan overheard him whisper, "I'm sorry, honey. I should have told you. We will be ready tomorrow. Okay?"

"Don't worry, daddy. I'll take care of everything like I always do."

Nova stood up. "I'll sleep on the couch, Callan. I don't want to put any more burden on you."

Callan laughed. "Nova, I have more than one bedroom. There is mine and two more. And just so you are more at peace, there are two full bathrooms. Come on. I'll show you where you can sleep and get some much-needed rest."

Nova inhaled. She was exhausted. So much needed to be handled before leaving tomorrow for the next racetrack. But for tonight, she and her dad were safe. Betty Boots had been fed and watered. Pulling the covers up, Nova closed her eyes. Her last thoughts were tomorrow a new day.

Sitting down on the couch, Callan leaned forward and massaged the back of his neck. What the hell just happened? Where did those two men appear from, and how much did Murray Cross owe them? Walking to his bedroom, Callan's last thoughts were she's just next door to me.

CHAPTER 1 1

Nova was running. They were behind her. They were going to catch her. There was no place to hide. There was nothing else to do. She screamed. She felt the arms. They were holding her. She could not breathe. She was terrified. With everything she could muster, Nova began fighting for her life.

It woke Callan from his slumber. He rubbed his eyes. What in the hell was going on? He heard it again. He knew it was Nova. Jumping up from the bed, he ran down the hallway and threw open the door. She was screaming. Callan knew she was having a nightmare. He did the only thing he could think of. He grabbed her and held her tight. He began patting her on his back. "Nova, it's me. It's Callan. You are safe. You are here with me. Nova, I am right here. Open your eyes, baby. Open your eyes and look at me."

Nova heard it. His voice. He was far away. Why could she not find him? Where was he? And then her body reacted on its own. He was holding her. He was telling her to open her eyes. He was here. He kept begging her to open her eyes. She did. He was looking at her with concern. There was something else. Without warning, Callan placed his hand on the side of her face. That small touch sent Nova over the edge. She was so tired. She was so tired of having to make decisions that would keep her and her father safe. She was exhausted from her father's bad choices in the industry. She couldn't hold it any longer. One tear found its way down Nova's cheek. She thought she could prevent more from trickling down. That was not the case. She began to cry.

Callan took his thumb and wiped away the first tear he saw. He felt Nova melt into him. He knew this feeling. He knew this emotion of just being overwhelmed. He knew that there was no solution, and the worse part was there was no end in sight. He did what he felt would help take her mind off her worries. Callan kissed her. He kissed her eyes where the tears were falling. He caught them with his lips. He kissed her lips. "Open, Nova. Open for me."

Nova did not want to think anymore. She only wanted to react to what she was feeling. She wanted Callan. She knew from that first meeting in the restaurant, there was an attraction. An emotion which she had never felt had taken over. Desire. Nova slowly opened her lips. She felt Callan's tongue. He was suckling her tongue. He was nibbling at Nova's lips as a treat.

Realizing the change in Nova, Callan pulled back. "Nova, now is the time to tell me to stop."

Nova knew what he was stating. If she did not tell him to stop, he would continue what? Nova could only imagine. In reality, she wanted more. She wanted Callan. It was only an act. There were no emotions involved. "Callan, I understand. I don't want to talk anymore about it. Please don't stop. Please don't leave me."

"I can promise you, Nova Cross, I have no plans of leaving you tonight."

Pulling her close to him, Callan began to kiss Nova. It was slow. He tugged at the corner of her lips. Nova nibbled back. Callan placed his hand on the side of her cheek. "Open for me, Nova. Open so I can taste you." Nova did as he asked. His tongue was gentle at first and then it became urgent. Callan felt the change in Nova's response to him. She leaned into Callan's chest. His chest was strong. It was strong enough to hold Nova's weight. She placed her hands on his chest. She felt his muscles underneath the t-shirt. "Callan, hold me."

Callan pulled her as tight as he could to him. "Nova, I'm here. I'm not going anywhere." He placed his finger under her chin and kissed her like a whisper on the wind. "Let me kiss your lips down to your tummy, Nova. Allow me to show you what I want to give you. I have to touch you, Nova. I cannot keep my hands to myself. Let me show you, Nova, what you are doing to me."

Nova could feel the heat rising in between her legs. She wanted to feel Callan's hands on her. What was happening? "Callan, I'm scared. I've never had this feeling before. I just don't need you, Callan, I want you. I want to feel you. When you touch me or even just graze my skin, a tingling sensation begins down there. I can't stop the feeling."

"Nova, trust me. Close your eyes. Wherever I touch you, return the touch. Let me learn your body. Let me teach you what I know. Let me guide you to the heavens."

"Yes, Callan, show me the heavens."

Callan pulled Nova's T-shirt over her head. He took his time. He kissed each breast as they were revealed to his lips.

Her arms reached high to remove her shirt entirely. Instinct made her cover her bra until he said no. "I want to see, Nova. Let me watch. Take your bra off, please. You cannot hide any longer. I want to see all of you. Do not close your eyes. I want you to see what you are doing to me."

Callan guided Nova's hand to his desire. "Do you feel that? That's what you do to me. That's the control you have over me." Nova inhaled. She had never heard these words before. "Tell me what to do next, Callan. Tell me what you want."

"You, Nova, I need to be inside of you. I need you to wrap your legs around my desire and not let go. Save me, Nova. Save me from my own torment of needing you. Let me show you."

Where the courage came from, Nova had no idea. She placed her hands on Callan's waist and slid his gym shorts down. He had nothing on underneath. Callan was nude. He stepped out. He cupped her butt. Slowly, Callan pulled her pj shorts down. Just like him, Nova was nude. Callan placed his finger on the tip of Nova and began to slowly tease her. Callan felt her tense. "Trust me, Nova."

Nova looked at Callan. "I do." That was all Callan needed to hear. "Then let me have all of you."

Callan laid Nova back on her bed. "I want to know every inch of your body, Nova. I want to be inside of you. I want you to feel all of me. Wrap your legs around me and let me enter your sweetness."

Nova did as Callan had asked. She felt the tip of Callan. He was doing small strokes around her clit. In and out but never fully entering her. It was agony. Nova could not handle the desire of not having Callan inside.

But her torment was to last a bit longer. Callan slowly pulled himself out. He slid up Nova's tummy with his tongue. He kissed her belly button and felt her tummy tighten.

Callan found what his tongue had been searching for. Nova's breasts. He began to massage the left breast with his hand. Taking the nipple between his fingers, Callan watched Nova. She arched her body towards Callan's tongue. He began to suckle the right breast until he could see the tautness. Nova was holding on to Callan's shoulder.

"Nova, tell me what you want me to do." Nova could not think straight. "Everything, Callan. I want you to do everything. My mind is spinning. My heart is beating faster than it ever has. It's you." Before she could change her mind, Nova reached for Callan's hardness. Gently rubbing, Nova felt him respond.

Nova guided Callan inside of her. "Callan, please don't stop. No more teasing. I can't wait any longer. Please let me feel you."

Callan needed her more than she knew. He pulled her forward and thrust inside. She was warm. She was moist to his entry. Callan pulled Nova's legs tighter around him. The friction. The heat. The release. Moving in and out, Callan watched as Nova placed her hand over mouth to quiet the moan of release. He felt the lips of Nova's clit tighten around him. It was all Callan could do to maintain control. Callan was hard. He could not wait any longer. The action made Callan out of control. He shuttered. Who was Nova Cross? And what spell had she placed on Callan Duncan?

CHAPTER 12

Callan gently laid his head on Nova's shoulder. He rolled to Nova's side. "Nova?" It was not a statement. It was a question.

"Callan. Thank you. I forgot what it was to feel the emotion and not the action. I do have a question, though."

Callan looked at Nova. A question after making love was never good. "Ask away."

Nova reached for Callan's necklace and allowed her hand to slide down his chest. "Tell me, Callan, tell me why this necklace and what it holds is so important to you. I never see you without it. And when you become concerned or nervous, you reach for it. I know there is a story. Please tell me."

Callan smiled. So, she had noticed. Not only that, but she had also inquired. Callan had never been asked that question. She was the first. Most of the time, he would push the charm and the coins around the back of his neck so they would not get in the way of his lovemaking. He did not stay long enough with a female for them to have time to even see the necklace, let alone have time to ask a question about it. But Nova had done just that.

"Nova, it's late. Let's both get some rest. In the morning, I promise to tell you the story."

Nova sensed he would not give into her begging. There was something mysterious about the way he protected the necklace and how he touched it. After what had just taken place, Nova hated to admit it. She was tired. Not physically, but emotionally. The day had been long. Her father's safety, along with Betty Boots' care, had taken its toll on Nova.

She didn't ask. She assumed he would. She kissed him and whispered, "good night, Callan Duncan" and turned to place her body in the outline of him. Callan had been prepared to leave his bedroom and go into the den to sleep on his couch. Evidently, that was not going to be the case. He liked the feel of Nova against his chest. As his eyes began to close, Callan did not want to think about tomorrow. Tomorrow would come with or without Callan revealing his story.

Nova was in a dream. She was safe. She was wrapped in love. No harm could befall her. It was euphoria. And then, she realized where she was and who was holding her. His breath was against her nude back. Another problem to worry about. She was nude. He was also. Nova could not face him. The emotions that she allowed him to see last night, the parts of her body that reacted to his touch. Her body had betrayed her. She had never experienced the need of such a desire. It was raw and she didn't know if she could explain it to Callan.

Callan knew she was awake. He would give her time. He did not want to rush her. He would wait until she was ready. He was enjoying her laying naked in his bed. He couldn't keep his thoughts from wondering what it would be like to wake up to Nova Cross like this every morning.

"Callan? Callan, are you awake? We need to get moving. I need to check on my father and then on Betty."

"I am Nova. I've been wide awake for a few minutes. I just wanted to give you time to wake up, as well. But before you leave me, though, look at me."

"No, Callan. I cannot."

"Why not? What's wrong?" Callan inquired.

"Well, if you must know, and I know you do because I can see you smiling even though I am not looking at you, that was not me last night."

Callan laughed. "Well, pray tell, honey, then who was it. Because I'm pretty sure you answered when I called your name. And I know of no other women named Nova."

"You're not going to let me move, are you? I'm going to have to turn around, and face you?"

"Yes, you are, Nova Cross. I know we have a million things to do, but this will only take a second. Look at me."

Nova did as Callan asked. She turned her body into his. She could not look at him. She placed her head on his shoulder. Callan kissed the top of her head. "Look at me, Nova. It's me. I did not change overnight. I'm still Callan Duncan and you are still Nova Cross, the daughter of Murray Cross, and the owner of Betty Boots."

Callan was watching for her reaction to his matter-of-fact statement. Nova licked her lips. "And, if you continue to do that, I can make no promises that I will not make love to you right here, right now. Worse will be the fact if your father wakes and finds you in my bedroom and not on the couch. I may just have to tell him how you threw your body at me and seduced me all night long."

Nova's eyes shot wide open, and she looked directly at Callan. "Callan, you would not?"

"No, sweetheart, I would not. I do have thoughts of how to keep you here longer, but I know there are matters we must attend to." Before she could respond, Callan leaned and kissed her. Her lips were soft and moist where she had been licking them. He pulled back. Her eyes were shadowy with desire. Why now? There was no time to play. "Enough, Nova. No more. We both need to move before neither of us can nor want to."

Nova knew he was serious. The tone of his voice was a dead giveaway. And just when Nova thought they had escaped being discovered, she heard her father's footsteps on the floor. "Nova, honey. Where are you?" And to make it even more unbelievable, she heard him say Callan's name, too.

Callan grinned. "I told you. Might as well as face the obvious. Nova, if you are worried, what your father will think, just tell him you had to go to the bathroom and did not want to wake him, so you came to mine."

Nova looked at Callan. "That's not bad. I think it will work, but only if I put my clothes on and you do, too!"

Callan rolled off to the other side of the bed. He threw on his t-shirt and shorts. "I'm good. I suggest you roll quickly to the other side and look at the floor where we tossed your t-shirt and shorts." Callan winked at her.

Nova looked at the floor. She grabbed her clothes and pulled them on. She ran to the bathroom. Callan closed the door and placed his hands on her lips. "I'll take care of your father. Can we be ready in fifteen minutes?"

Nova without hesitation kissed Callan. "Thank you and yes."

Nova could hear Callan and her father talking about what else but the industry. She could hear the pride in her father's voice when he spoke about how they had come to own Betty Boots. But what made Nova stop before she opened the bedroom door was Callan's voice. Asking questions, inquiring about her father's life before Nova, requesting his insight on the races today. Who was this man she had made love to last night? Not only that, but he had also yet to tell her the story of the necklace and the coins, and why they were so precious to him.

Opening the door, she cleared her throat. "I'm ready, if you are."

Callan winked at her. "I see. And yes, I am ready. Your father has decided to stay behind and get some rest. I told him to review the next stop we would make and see who Betty Boot's competition was.

Nova caught that last inference to the words "next stop" and raised her eyebrow.

Callan touched Nova's arm. "Grab your bag, Nova. We will talk in the truck on the drive over. Okay?"

Callan looked back at Murray. He knew Mr. Cross needed this time away from the trouble that had been revealed. Callan also knew that he needed time to assess the trouble and how to help Nova. The truck ride would be very interesting.

Nova closed the truck door and buckled herself in. "First, thank you for taking care of dad. Second, I heard the words 'next stop' and third, you owe me an explanation."

Callan could not help but chuckle. "I didn't think you would let me off so easy. Is it the necklace and the coins? You want to know why they are so special to me?"

"I do," Nova smiled.

"Well, the three coins have a special year on them. The year my father was born. The year my mother was born. And the year I was born."

"And the necklace, Callan. I know there is something written on it. I think I know what it says."

Callan automatically reached to touch the necklace and coins. "It only says the word 'lucky'."

"Like the ink on your arm. It's rather unusual, because the tattoo is in cursive," Nova told him.

"Yes, it is my mother's handwriting. When she passed, I had it tattooed on my arm. Just a special memory of her I keep and the saying she told me about my father."

Nova could not help it. "Please tell me, Callan. Why the word 'lucky'?"

Callan could not remember the last time he had shared his mother's story of love for his father. It was few and far between that he revealed the truth. "She told me she used to believe that there was no such thing as luck. Life and love were a gamble. But, when she met my father, she was lucky in the gamble she took with my father. There are no guarantees,

Nova, when it comes to love. My mother told me as their relationship developed, she knew that luck had brought them together. The gamble was the life they made together. It never faltered. It never failed. Their love remained steadfast."

Nova listened to Callan's voice and how it changed when he spoke of his parents. "Thank you, Callan. Thank you for sharing. One day, I hope to be lucky just like your mom."

Pulling into the track, Callan could not help but think, she already was. She just had no idea.

CHAPTER 13

Callan could not take his eyes off of Nova. From the moment, Betty Boots sensed Nova's presence, Betty had not stopped whinnying. Nova had placed peppermints in her pocket to coax Betty on to the trailer.

On the drive over, Nova and Callan had discussed what must be done regarding Murray and regarding the continuing season for Betty.

They both agreed that the best place for Murray was in Callan's home. It was off the beaten path. Murray would have time to do nothing. There were no worries about day-to-day events. This would allow Murray to receive much needed mental rest as physical rest. It would also take the stress off of Nova. Nova needed to concentrate on Betty and her next race.

"Callan, Betty Boots and I are ready. Did you already hitch the trailer to your truck? The sooner we return home, the better with time and distance for tomorrow's arrival."

Callan caught the slip of the word "home". He was pretty sure, Nova did not. He didn't mind it, though. "The sooner we return home" and the inference that she considered it her home sounded good to Callan.

"Yes, the truck is parked outside, around the corner. What can I help with?"

"Nothing, I just need to place the bridle over her head and lead her out. She's been fed and given her treat. She should be good to go. I'll do it, okay. She doesn't know you and I don't want to spook her."

Callan nodded. He understood routine. It was essential, not just with humans, but with animals, as well. He stood by the corner of the truck and listened to the encouraging words and support that Nova was giving Betty Boots. He watched as Nova led Betty out of the stall and to the trailer. Preparing to load Betty in, Betty stopped and looked directly at Callan. Callan knew Betty Boots sensed that this was not Mr. Murray Cross. He wanted to reach out to pet Betty, but he did not have to. Betty dipped her head into Callan's shoulders as if she were encouraging him in this adventure.

A tear formed. She had never seen Betty Boots do the nuzzle lean with anyone other than her father. Evidently, Betty knew that Callan Duncan was someone special.

Nova double checked the back of the trailer. Making sure Betty was standing where she needed, Nova leaned around the corner of the trailer. "Let's do this, Mr. Duncan."

Arriving at his home, Callan saw Murray sitting on the front porch in the rocking chair. The rocker had been handed down from his grandfather to his father and then from Callans' father to Callan. It was more than 50 years old. "He looks good, Callan. Thank you for offering your home to my dad until you and I return and get matters all squared away and issues handled with dollars," Nova stated.

Murray had his eyes closed. He heard the truck pull in the driveway. He would need to figure out now he and Nova would pay the debt and finish out the season. It had been weighing on his mind all morning.

Instead of wasting time sitting and waiting for Callan and Nova, Murray stood up and began the long walk to the truck. As they both stepped out, Murray looked at Nova. "Honey, we need to talk about yesterday and put a plan into motion for the remainder of ...." That was as far as Murray Cross got.

"Dad, Callan, and I have made the best decision for you and for Betty Boots. We are here to pack. You will remain here at Callan's home. We will be back in six weeks. You do not need to leave the safety of Callan's home. As a matter of fact, I am taking the keys to our truck. We will have delivery set up for you by the local grocery. I am not asking you, daddy. I am telling you this is where you are going to reside until Callan, and I return from the circuit and finish out the season with Betty."

Murray's eyes opened wide with shock. "Callan, did you agree to this or are you just now hearing this?"

Callan could not help but laugh at the question. Callan pointed his finger in Nova's direction. "I promise you, Murray, I am in total agreement with her. She only twisted my arm a bit."

"Don't you dare. Both you and I agreed this was the best for daddy and for Betty. Don't make me look like the bad guy. As for you daddy, I'm only asking for you to behave for six weeks. I need to get business taken care of and the only way to do this is to take Callan with Betty Boots and me. You're all I got. This is the best decision for all of us."

Murray knew his daughter was correct. He hated that he had placed them both in a position that Nova would be without him. He didn't know why, but he needed to. He reached out his hand towards Callan. "Take good care of her. She's my entire life, Callan. I promise I will stay here. I need your word you will not allow any harm to come to my girls."

Callan placed his hand in Murray's. "Mr. Cross, please do not worry. Your girls will be safe and well cared for. My word is the only thing I have. I could tell you not to worry, but you will. Six weeks, Mr. Cross. That's all Nova, Betty Boots and I need. We will return in six weeks."

There was no time to waste. Callan walked into his bedroom and reached underneath. He pulled it out. It had dust on it. He had not used it since his grandfather had passed. Callan smiled. The suitcase had been handed down from grandfather, to father, to Callan. Placing it on the bed, Callan packed what he thought he would need in order to make that first impression. The circuit was tight. All knew who would be arriving next. Whether it was the horse or whether it was a new player to the game.

Callan walked out. Nova was standing there. There was nothing in her hand. There was nothing laying at her feet. It was only Nova.

Without thinking, Callan raised an eyebrow. "Honey, where is your suitcase?"

Nova grinned. "Not to worry, Mr. Duncan. All that I own has been hidden this entire time in the back of Betty

Boots' trailer. I appreciate your concern, but we must be at the Pennyrile racetrack in the next four hours and unload."

Callan knew she was right. He handed Murray the keys to his home. "I made a promise to you. Both your girls will be safe and taken care of."

Nova overheard the last few words. She walked towards her father. Murray pulled her in for a hug. "Remember, the old saying, Nova - Hoping to recoup is what ruins the gambler. Be wise, honey. Be careful. But most importantly, don't fall in love with him."

Nova kissed her father on the side of his cheek and whispered in his ear. "It's too late."

She stepped back from her father's embrace and knew that the next steps she would take would create a new journey for her. Would this opportunity allow her to see a different side of the circuit? As she looked in on Betty Boots to be sure she was doing okay, she felt it. His stare. He was watching and waiting. Nova looked at Callan. "I'm good. Let's do this."

Callan thought to himself that backing down the driveway was not going to be the most difficult part of this trip. It was knowing what was going to happen and what the outcome would be. Callan would protect Nova and he would be sure that Betty Boots would win, but who was going to protect him?

CHAPTER 14

Rolling over, one eye open, trying to read the clock through glazed eyes, Nova knew it would be time to rise. Five weeks had passed quickly. One more circuit to run. One more track. One more week with Callan Duncan. Nova could not have asked for a better chaperone. Callan was just that. A chaperone.

When they had left to run the circuit, Callan asked Nova if she would be okay sharing a room with him while they were travelling. It would cut down on expenses. Nova could not argue that fact. Nova also did not have to worry that Callan would attempt anything else other than just to sleep and dress and head to the racetrack with her.

She could not erase the thought from her mind. Had she done something that Callan did not like the first time they made love. Was he disappointed in her experience? Why had he not touched Nova these five weeks. There had been every opportunity and yet, he would offer a congratulatory hug when Betty won her race. Callan would even kiss her on the side of her cheek. But that was it. There was nothing else. It was as if that one night had never occurred. That night had been wiped clean from the slates. It was only a memory. Nothing more, nothing less.

Brushing her teeth, Nova heard Callan. Before he could say anything, she told him she was finishing, and he could have the bathroom in less than two minutes.

"Take your time. We need to pack, get a quick bite to eat and head to the track. Did you remember to get Betty a treat?"

Nova smiled. Betty Boots had taken a liking to receiving special attention and treats from Callan. And from what Nova could surmise from their attachment, Callan enjoyed treating Betty special.

"Yes, sir. I have them. They are in the truck."

"Good, as soon as the race is over, we will collect our winnings and begin the long trip home. We may have to stay overnight depending on the time we leave, but we should be back home in less than forty-eight hours. I know Murray misses you. We've been away long enough. The winnings should be enough to pay for the debt owed with a few dollars left over."

Nova was listening. She felt a weird sensation in her stomach. For six weeks, her entire life had been wrapped around Betty Boots and Callan Duncan. What would Nova return to?

The bathroom door opened. Callan looked at Nova. It had taken every ounce of his willpower not to touch her. He had only given her a hug, and it wasn't even a real hug. There was no embracing. There was no holding onto Nova. Hell, Callan had only kissed her on the cheek. If she knew what was racing through Callan's mind every time he saw her step through a doorway, or if she even knew he pretended to sleep so that he could watch her sleep, she would be embarrassed. He had made a promise to Murray. He would keep the promise, no matter the times he would have liked to have thrown caution to the wind.

But this morning was the realization there would be no more mornings such as this. Knowing that she was a part of his day. Knowing that when they returned, their lives would resume as before. And with the one thought lingering, Callan said screw it. He stood up and stopped in front of Nova. "You are beautiful, Nova Cross." Callan kissed her on the lips. The kiss was not meant to last.

Nova was taken aback. She had to reach for Callan's waist to steady herself. This kiss was different. It was not like the first time they met. Nova needed that feeling. She kissed Callan back.

Callan sensed it. He could not deny it any longer. All the restraint in the world could not take away his desire nor his need for Nova. "Nova, let me taste what I have craved these last weeks."

Nova did as he asked. It was such a simple request and one that she was willing to do. His tongue teased inside Nova. He placed his hands on Nova's waist and pulled her closer. "This is what you do to me. Every time I am near you. I cannot control it any longer, Nova. I want you."

Nova did not want to think about Betty Boots. She did not want to worry about her father. She did not want to be responsible for the debt. What she did want was Callan Duncan.

"Callan, I cannot hold back any longer. I want you too. I want to feel you. I have missed your touch. Please don't let go."

That was all Callan needed to hear. He began to unbutton Nova's blouse. He slid the blouse down her arms. He undid the button of her jeans. Slowly, he unzipped and shimmied them down. Nova did not have panties on. She was nude from the waist down. "Step out, Nova, please."

As she stepped out, Callan took his hands on the inside of Nova's legs and traced a path to where he knew heaven could be found. He took his time kissing the inside of her legs. His tongue led Callan to her. He needed to taste Nova. Callan heard Nova inhaling. Nova reached for the top of Callan's head to steady herself. She was going to crumble should Callan continue. Nova's body was responding in ways she never knew she could feel.

Callan felt Nova shiver. He knew she had found satisfaction with the last thrust of his tongue. Callan shuddered. If felt incredible to feel her release. He was concerned that it had to be so quick. He was sad he could not take his time and linger in the warmth of Nova. But Betty Boots needed Nova and so did Callan. Today was the day that would set both he and Nova back on the path of routine before they had ever met that day in the restaurant.

Races are good. At least that's what Callan's father had stood by. Callan only prayed that this last race, this last run on the circuit, would take them to the finish line. Pulling into the backside of the track, Callan could sense that Nova was anxious. He turned towards Nova to tell her he understood her nervousness. Hell, he was nervous, too. He knew what was at stake. Before he could say the first word, Nova reached for his hand. She squeezed Callan's hand lightly.

"Callan, I can never say thank you enough. I do not know how to express the words of what you have done, not just for me or Betty Boots, but for my father. You have literally saved our family from financial ruin. I don't know how to repay you."

Callan knew she was sincere. There was nothing fake about Nova. Not even her hair. These last six weeks, Nova had presented herself in a very professional, business manner. She always wore her hair in a slick back coiffure. Her hair was not long but it held the sleek ponytail look. Her makeup was not dramatic but more natural. Her fingernails were kept manicured with a soft pink polish. Callan looked at Nova. Even if Nova tried to be someone else, she could not. It was not in her genes.

"Nova, thank you. Just one more. Just one more race today and then we can head home and back to some type of normalcy and even a routine. You still trust me?"

Nova laughed and nodded. "How in the world could you ask that question? For six weeks, I have been in your presence and knowledge of this industry. And this morning was your only lapse in judgment." Nova winked.

Callan knew what she was referencing. Nova did have a playful side to her. "Nova, my sweetheart, there was no lapse. It was meant to happen. If not, I was going to make it happen."

Parking and opening her door, Callan stopped in front of her. "This will be great day. She will win and we are going home."

Nova kissed him. Not on the cheek. But on Callan's lips. It was not sexual. She wanted it to mean something. It was permanent. She hoped Callan did not know. Nova was in love with him. Was love truly a gamble? From Nova's perspective, love was unknown and needed time to be discovered. Six weeks had proven this to Nova. Nova would gamble on Callan any day.

CHAPTER 15

As they were walking towards Betty Boots' stall, Callan sensed rather than saw. The two men that had words with Murray were standing over to the side, leaning against their vehicle. Callan gave a small head nod. He wanted them to know that he had seen them. They returned the nod.

Before Nova could say anything, Callan ushered her into the barn. "Let's check on Betty Boots and Gavin. He has done well with her. He knows her pace, Nova. He allows her to lead."

Nova couldn't help it. "Just as every man should with a female. We do know directions better than you guys."

Callan threw his hands in the air. "Directions with a vehicle, yes, but on other matters, I am pretty damn good. I listen really well to wants and needs."

Callan saw Gavin walking towards them. He waited til he got close. "Morning, Gavin. Everything good?"

In these last six weeks, Gavin was appreciative of the fact of being able to ride Betty Boots, but more than anything, Callan and Nova had made an impression on him. Gavin knew these two were destined to be together whether they wanted to admit it or not.

Walking into the track to find their seats, Callan placed his hand on Nova's back. "She's ready. Gavin is ready. One more, Nova. One more win."

Callan looked around. The two men had followed them inside. They were sitting behind Nova and Callan. Again, Callan wanted them to know he had seen them. He turned to look at them. One tipped his finger to Callan as an acknowledgement.

The biggest race was the last. The last race was the one for the big money. It was all or nothing. This was the one that Betty Boots needed to win. There was no room for place or show. It had to be the big "W". The win.

Settling into their seats, Callan listened as the horses were called to the starting gate. It had been a long day. He could tell Nova was exhausted. Callan stood up. Nova stood and leaned into Callan's shoulders. She needed those shoulders to hold her up. "I'm scared, Callan. There is no second or third, she must be first."

Callan kissed the top of Nova's head. "She knows, Nova. Gavin knows. It will happen."

Nova held her breath. Betty Boots and Gavin came off that curve like a blast of dynamite. She was in the lead. Only two horses were close enough to catch her. They were hanging around Betty like those old horse flies. Never leaving. Aggravating as hell. One on each side. And then it happened, Betty Boots leaned for the win. It was by a nose. Nova screamed. Callan picked her up and held her tight. He slid her body down his. Her lips were less than a breath away from his. Callan kissed Nova. This kiss was different than most. This kiss was different than the others he had given. This kiss was a kiss of promise.

Heading to the winner's circle, Nova could not help but let a few tears flow. "Callan, you saw them, didn't you? I do not know when they arrived, but I saw them when I sat down. They were sitting behind us, weren't they? Please don't lie to me."

Callan whispered into her ear so only she could hear. "Yes, I saw them. They are still here. I will take care of repaying Murray's debt and then I will make sure they leave and never bother you and your father again. Let's gather our winnings and then let's get rid of the debt and send them packing."

"Thank you, Callan. Thank you for making sure my father and I would be protected and safe."

Walking towards the barn, Gavin approached them. Nova ran to him and hugged him. She handed Gavin an envelope. "This is for you. Thank you for all that you have done with Betty Boots. There's a little extra in there. We are headed home, Gavin. If you need me to speak to another trainer on your behalf, please let me know. My daddy and I will always be here for you."

Gavin took the envelope. He hugged Miss Nova and then shook Callan's hand.

One more matter to handle, and they would be on the road. Nova looked at Callan. "I can do it. I can pay them off. Daddy told me the amount, the amount of the debt, Callan."

Callan laughed. "I am not afraid of them, Nova. They've been waiting for us since the race ended. They are in their truck. They have been watching this entire exchange between you and Gavin. Hand me the envelope. I'll make sure we all see eye to eye and the debt is repaid and never to come near you or Murray again."

Nova nodded. "Here it is. The amount that daddy told me. We only have a little bit leftover, but it's something to start with." Callan took the envelope and began the walk over towards the two men's truck. He held his hand up. As he approached the truck, Callan began with "Guys, there is no need to get out of your vehicle. Here is all that is due and owing. I want you to count it inside your vehicle and agree with me that Murray Cross and Nova Cross will never be contacted again. The debt is repaid."

Nova watched him walk across that parking lot. He was taking forever. She had seen the truck drive away with those men inside. Callan had stood there for what seemed eternity. Callan was taking his ever-loving sweet time. She started to take the step towards him. Callan could tell she was worried. He knew she had never stood that still in one place the entire time they had been racing. He walked towards her. "Nova, they are gone. The debt is repaid. There is nothing to worry about. They will not be bothering you or Murray anymore."

And just like that, the day had ended. The race had been won. Winnings collected. Debts paid. It was time to go home.

CHAPTER 16

Nova had made the call to her dad. They were on their way back home. The problem had been taken care of. She had a few bucks left in her pocket. Betty Boots had done magnificently. She did not want her father to know all that hand transpired between her and Callan. So, she told her father that Callan was a true gentleman. No need to raise her father's concern about anything else.

Callan was driving and listening to Nova's conversation with Murray, a dangerous combination. He loved hearing her say "Dad, he was true gentleman, the entire time. I promise, the entire time."

Nova knew he was listening. She gave Callan a stern look and placed her fingers on his lips. "Not a word," she told him in a hushed voice.

Less than five miles. They would be home in less than five minutes. He looked over at Nova. She was asleep. The passenger seat reclined. She had tried to stay awake for the entire drive, but Callan knew she needed rest. The trailer was empty. They had stopped and returned Betty Boots back to Whitney Stables and her stall where she would remain for a couple of days until Nova and her father decided what the next step would be on the circuit. Betty Boots also deserved a much-needed rest.

Pulling into his driveway, Callan saw him. There he was sitting on the porch as if it were just a routine night. Callan smiled. He liked Murray. He also knew that he did not like Nova. He was in love with Nova. She was worth the gamble he had taken.

Murray rose. There they were. His heart was pounding so fast. They were home. His baby girl, Nova, was safe. She was back. Callan had kept his promise.

Placing the truck in park, Callan waited for Nova to wake. She moaned and placed her hand over her eyes. "Are we home, Callan? Do you see daddy?"

"He's walking towards us, Nova. We are home."

Nova sat up. There was Callan's home. There was her dad. She unbuckled her seat belt and flung the door open. She jumped out and began to run up the driveway. Her father held his arms open. Nova jumped into her dad's arms and wrapped hers tightly around his neck. With a whisper like the wind on a warm night, Nova told her dad, "No more, daddy. We will be discussing a new game plan."

Callan breathed a sigh of relief. They were home.

CHAPTER 17

Callan could not believe it. The aroma of breakfast. He could smell the bacon. He could hear the potatoes frying. He could hear her voice speaking with her dad. The last morning with Nova and Murray.

Murray had sat up with Callan last night talking about the last six weeks and all that occurred. Callan could tell that Murray was very proud of Nova. Callan also knew that Murray was ready to relax and possibly the other "R" word, retire from the circuit.

Callan walked out of his bedroom. Murray had insisted that Callan rest in his own bed, his own room. Callan was too tired to argue with Murray. It was late. Callan watched Nova at the stove. Murray was at the table reading the program book for the day. Without worrying about the repercussions or outcome, Callan kissed Nova on the cheek and said, "good morning".

Nova was taken aback but she did not want her dad to make a big deal, or it would become the hot topic for discussion. "Good morning, Callan. Go ahead and sit down and I'll fix your plate."

Callan chuckled. "With pleasure. I'm starving."

Murray watched the exchange between both. He and Nova would need to leave sooner rather than later. They needed to get back to a routine with just him and Nova.

Murray cleared his throat. "Callan, both Nova and I can never say thank you. All that you have done for us and for Betty Boots is truly appreciated. But we will be leaving today. We will be heading back home with Betty tonight. We don't need to waste or occupy any more of your time." Murray pushed his chair back from the table. "Nova, when you are finished eating breakfast, let's get on the road. There's no time like the present to begin a new journey. I've already packed what I had when we arrived, which was nothing major. Go ahead and shower and we will get on the road before we have overstayed our welcome any longer."

Callan wanted to object for Nova to take her time. He knew that would not be the case. Callan informed Nova he would clean up and for her to go ahead and take her shower. Callan did not want to delay them any longer with getting on the road.

Nova could not look at Callan. She was not ready to leave. She had an empty feeling in her stomach.

Within less than an hour, Callan's house was back to what it had been. Quiet. Callan had watched as Nova backed the truck with the trailer down the driveway. It took less than five minutes for her to disappear. To disappear from his life. Did the last six weeks even exist? Was what he had felt for Nova 'a just because' relationship. They had been thrown together because of a unique issue and that's all the relationship had developed from – the issue. The issue was now resolved. It no longer existed. Everything would return to normal, right?

This was the first week of heading back to the restaurant. He genuinely missed Jimmy and Allie. He could not wait to tell them of his journeys. They would never believe him. He stood in front of the bathroom mirror. He reached for the necklace. Yes, they were still there. Three coins and the medallion. Routine was what he needed. There was nothing wrong with just being normal, was there? To have the same routine over and over. It was security, the routine was not supposed to change. Why change the routine, right?

Walking out the front door, Callan stopped. He needed to be needed. It was okay to be dull and boring. Callan headed to where he would be safe. The restaurant.

Three months had passed. He wondered about her. He wondered about him. Were they doing, okay? There had been no talk of Betty Boots running at any of the tracks. There had been no talk of Murray Cross or even her.

Callan had thought about trying to find her. But he could not do it. She needed time to take care of her father. He needed time to get over her.

Opening the door to the restaurant, he could see from the window, Jimmy and Allie had a full house.

Allie looked up. She motioned with her hand for Callan to sit at the bar. Allie hollered at Jimmy. "Callan's here, go ahead and fix his usual." Jimmy hollered back at Allie. "Sugar, I saw him come in. Already on it."

In the last few months, Jimmy and Allie had become become a permanent fixture in Callan's day-to-day activities. Always giving Callan free advice, even when none was needed.

Allie handed him the program. "Here you go. Nothing important that I can see, but you may see something I did not."

Callan laughed. "I trust you, Miss Allie. You know as much, if not more, than me when it comes to the industry."

Allie placed his plate on the bar with his coffee. "I am much more knowledgeable, aren't I? But for today you're ahead of the game this morning. Enjoy your meal."

Callan had his back to the door. All morning it had been opening and closing like a revolving door at a hotel establishment. Callan knew several of the regulars. Some, of course, were tourists. Just stopping in to check out the restaurant and learn a bit more about the industry. Business as usual.

The restaurant door opened again. The wind blew in the scent. A scent he knew. A scent he recognized. A scent he loved. He did not want to believe it. It could not be. There was no way it was. Callan turned. There was no one there.

Callan turned back around. And then he heard it. The high heel shoes hitting the hardwood floor. He could not turn around. He could not handle any more disappointment anymore. What if it were not who he thought it was? There it was, her scent.

And, then it happened, the touch. He tilted his head without turning around and began with a question, "Nova?"

The drive to the restaurant was taking too long. She could not get there quick enough. She had to do it before she chickened out. If she thought more about it, she would not do it. He had to know. He had to realize.

"Yes, Callan, it's me. Look at me, please."

Before he could respond, Nova turned Callan in the bar chair, so he was facing her. "I'm here, Callan."

Callan noticed she was by herself. "Nova, where is your father? Is Murray with you?"

"No, he is home, Callan. He decided it was time to retire and teach the younger versions of him how to read a program book and how to learn more about the industry of horseracing. The beauty as well as the downfalls. Education in this industry is something that can be taught as well as inherited."

"Nova, before anything else is said, you must know. You cannot be that blind and not know what took place while we were together."

Nova smiled. "Can you not say it, Callan. Because if you cannot, I will. I love you."

Callan raised his eyebrows. "You love me, Miss Cross? I guess there's only one thing to say. Love is a gamble. I'm ready to gamble.

EPILOGUE

"Nova, did you get the last order? Make sure that the toast is on white.

"Callan Duncan, my love, I heard you loud and clear. I am not deaf, and I am not that old that I need hearing aids. Again, I hear you loud and clear."

"Miss Allie, do you hear how not just the co-owner of the restaurant is speaking to me, but my wife, as well", Callan pleaded.

Jimmy chuckled. "Son don't plead your case. You don't have a case. She is the co-owner. She is your wife. She is always right. The sooner you learn this, the better your life will be."

"Whoa, you two. You guys have not been married long enough to take sides. You've only been married two more months than Nova and me. You guys need to enjoy your breakfast that was made with love and allow us to make mistakes so we can come to you for advice," Nova laughed.

Nova searched the restaurant for his spot. "Dad are you ready. They are waiting in the back. It's a good crowd. A lot of tourists, dad. Be gentle. Go slow. Like you told me, the goal is they learn the entire industry."

Murray stated, "Nova, honey, I got this. Quit worrying and get back to managing the restaurant with that husband of yours."

Callan came up behind Nova. "Best decisions we ever made were hiring Jimmy's son as the grill chef and Allie's granddaughters as waitresses. I know it was a gamble, but they have turned out really well."

"Callan Duncan, I thought you had given up gambling?"

"Nova Cross, my bet will always be on you. I thought love would be a gamble. It's not love until you take the gamble. I am a gambler. I am a lover. You have the best of both worlds. Gamble with me, Nova, and let me show you love. I'm glad you did not listen to Murray that one day. The gamble was never love. The gamble was me."

Nova pulled Callan close to her. "I will take that gamble," Mr. Duncan.

ABOUT THE AUTHOR

Cook Studio

de de Cox

Kentucky Romance Author

The Day You Go from Romance Junkie to # 1 Best-Selling Kentucky Romance Author

de de began pursuing her dream of becoming a romance author at the age of 30. Born and raised on the farm in Rooster Run, Kentucky, de de was raised on the core values of the 3Cs (kindness, caring, and compassion). Throughout her young adulthood, de de volunteered in the community with her family, and specifically, her grandmother, Bea. Growing up in the country, romance novels were her escape to another world. de de knew that one day, her dream of writing a romance novel would come true. Fast forward to 2018, when de de picked the book back up that she had begun in her early 30s. As in life, circumstances and direction change the course, BUT never the ending goal. Learning the industry and working with her publisher, Beyond Global Publishing, God opened many doors and many connections, and de de has never looked back.

de de became a published Kentucky romance author in 2018. She is the #1 best-selling Kentucky romance author of the Two Degrees Series, which features her son, Bo, as the male model. Little did de de know that her child would become the next FabiBo.

de de has now completed twelve (12) romance books and lucky #13 is ready to debut. A Bridled Affair – When Love is a Gamble debuts April 13, 2024 (just in time for the 150th Kentucky Derby).

de de has served as a board member of The Dream Factory of Louisville, KY, Opal's Dream Foundation, Spalding University – Athletic Board, as well as volunteered with other charitable entities. de de received the coveted 2018 Spirit of Louisville Foundation - WLKY Bell Award for her volunteerism within her community and now serves on the board as trustee.

de de is active within the pageant industry. She is the co-director of the Miss Hillview, Miss Buttermilk, and Miss Iron Horse Rolling Fork prelim pageants – all part of the Kentucky State Festival pageant system.

FAMILY (family always mean I love you) and this is true in de de's life. So many kind-hearted folk have traveled the journey. She has been married over 35 years to her best friend, Scott, from high school. She has two sons and one rotten feline (Sunny).

de de encourages others to live by HIS word – Acts 20:35.

Milton Keynes UK
Ingram Content Group UK Ltd.
UKHW020629210424
441426UK00006B/39